S0-CYD-607

Halloween Danny

written and photographed
by
Mia Coulton

It was Halloween night.

3

Danny put on a witch hat.

It   was   too   pointed.

He   put

on   a   football   uniform.

It was too tight.

He put

rabbit ears on his head.

They were too floppy.

Danny looked in the mirror.

"Woof, woof," barked Danny.

He liked what he saw.

Happy   Halloween!